The main character of this tale is a very sweet animal that lives in China. The giant panda is one of the species classified as "vulnerable" by the IUCN (International Union for Conservation of Nature).

XUAN LOC XUAN

GIANT
a Panda of the Enchanted Forest

Happy Fox BOOKS

He lay cozily on the tree branch, letting his legs dangle.
He yawned and fell asleep.

Giant woke up the next morning and started thinking about this forest, his home now. There were some other animals around, but Giant liked being on his own.

He spoke only to the bamboos and mostly to Big Trunk,
a tall reed rising from the middle of the forest.
Giant shared his secrets and dreams with Big Trunk.

Later that morning Giant took a nap and began to dream. Childhood memories filled his mind. He dreamed of his mother's warm hugs and the fun he had playing with Bino, his twin brother.

Giant dreamed of the days and days it took to walk to this forest.

In his dream, he remembered the first time he had seen the village and the people who lived there. He knew they loved his forest, too. Even people from far away came to see the forest—and Giant.

The tourists took photos of him!

"Giant!" a voice suddenly yelled, waking Giant from his dream. He looked around, but saw no one. "Get up! Right now!" He looked down—nothing. He looked up—nothing. Whose voice was that?

"It's me—Big Trunk."
Giant stammered,
"You c-c-can t-t-talk!"
"Only if necessary,"
replied Big Trunk,
"and in this case,
it's very necessary."

Recovering from his shock, Giant asked, "Where's all this heat coming from? The sun is not yet high in the sky."

Giant climbed down from the branch and ran to the edge of the forest.
"Help! Help!" he shouted.
The villagers didn't hear him.
The flames were already spreading.

He turned to Big Trunk and asked, "What should we do now?"
"Use the villagers' bamboo sled to carry wet sand to the fire. Throw it at the fire to put it out," suggested Big Trunk.

Giant did as he was told.
But the flames were much too high
to be put out by sand.

Panting, he cried out, "Big Trunk, it's not enough. The sand isn't working!"
"Try water. Use bamboo to make a big hose that can bring the water from the lake."

Giant worked quickly. He stuck one end of the bamboo hose into the lake and dragged the other end close to the flames. But the jet was too weak and the fire too strong.

"Big Trunk, Big Trunk, nothing is working! Look, the fire has already taken over most of the forest. Only the villagers can save it now."
"Poke holes in me," commanded Big Trunk.
"What do you mean?" asked Giant in shock.
"No time to explain; poke holes all the way down my trunk!"
"But won't that hurt you?"
"The most important thing is to try to save you and my bamboo brothers."

Giant bent Big Trunk down and dug holes with his long claws. He could see that Big Trunk was in pain, but he didn't hear a single cry.

The wind passing through the holes whistled and hissed. Like a gigantic pipe, Big Trunk made sounds so loud that they could be heard from miles away. The other bamboos joined in the alarm by rustling their thin leaves and banging against each other's hollow reeds.

The villagers heard the bamboos' alarm. Someone began shouting. People were pointing at the forest.

Giant and the villagers fought the fire for hours.

Finally, they succeeded in putting out the fire. The forest was saved.

Giant looked down at his sooty fur and decided to take a bath.

He saw his reflection in the water. But how was this possible? His fur looked clean. He gazed closer and realized that there were two figures: the soot-covered one was him, and there was another panda looking down from a nearby tree.

**Then Giant recognized the panda.
"Bino, is that really you?" cried Giant.
"Yes! It's been a long time, hasn't it?"
replied his twin brother, climbing down the tree.
Bino and Giant hugged each other with so much joy.**

"But how did you find me?" asked Giant.
"After Mama died, I started looking for you. I walked for weeks, and just when I had lost all hope, I heard strange sounds coming from this forest. Who was making those sounds?"

Giant led his brother to the middle of the forest. There among the other bamboos was Big Trunk. The holes made by Giant had turned into smiles.

Happy Fox Books is an imprint of Fox Chapel Publishing Company, Inc., 903 Square Street, Mount Joy, PA 17552.

© 2018 Snake SA, Chemin du Tsan du Péri 10, 3971 Chermignon, Switzerland

Giant: A Panda of the Enchanted Forest is an original work, first published in North America in 2018 by Fox Chapel Publishing Company, Inc. Reproduction of its contents is strictly prohibited without written permission from the rights holder.

ISBN 978-1-64124-014-7

Library of Congress Cataloging-in-Publication Data

Names: Xuan, Xuan Loc, author, illustrator.
Title: Giant : a panda of the Enchanted Forest / Xuan Loc Xuan.
Other titles: Gigante il panda della Foresta Incantata. English
Description: Mount Joy : Happy Fox Books, 2018. | Originally published: Chermignon, Switzerland : Snake SA, 2018 under the title, Gigante il panda della Foresta Incantata. | Summary: "A young panda named Giant befriends a wise bamboo named Big Trunk and they work together to save the forest from fire"-- Provided by publisher.
Identifiers: LCCN 2018012854 | ISBN 9781641240147 (hardcover)
Subjects: | CYAC: Giant panda--Fiction. | Pandas--Fiction. | Bamboo--Fiction. | Forest fires--Fiction. | China--Fiction.
Classification: LCC PZ7.1.X83 Gi 2018 | DDC [E]--dc23
LC record available at https://lccn.loc.gov/2018012854

To learn more about the other great books from Fox Chapel Publishing, or to find a retailer near you, call toll-free 800-457-9112 or visit us at *www.FoxChapelPublishing.com*.

We are always looking for talented authors. To submit an idea, please send a brief inquiry to acquisitions@foxchapelpublishing.com.

Fox Chapel Publishing makes every effort to use environmentally friendly paper for printing.

Printed in China

First printing

Pandas' forest homes are threatened in many ways, including the construction of roads and railways through their habitat, the widespread harvesting of bamboo and medicinal herbs, and the increase in tourists and related industries in the forests. Learn how you can help pandas survive and thrive by visiting online resources such as *www.worldwildlife.org* or *www.pandasinternational.org*.

XUAN LOC XUAN

Born in a village in Vietnam, she studied graphic design at the prestigious Ho Chi Minh City University of Fine Arts. In her art she shows themes related to nature, using a light and delicate touch. She is a freelance illustrator living in Ho Chi Minh City, Vietnam.